Published by Amazon's Kindle Direct Publishing

First paperback edition April 2023.

Written and Illustrated by Joe Lampe.

ISBN: 9798391988182

The
(Totally Appropriate)
Shirt

Alphabet

Aa

Ape shirt

Bb

Bull shirt

Cc

cow shirt

Dd

Dip shirt

Ee

Eat shirt

Ff

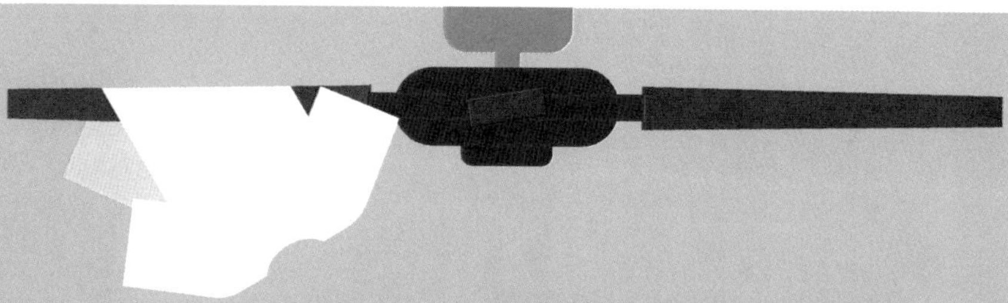

Shirt hit the **f**an

Gg

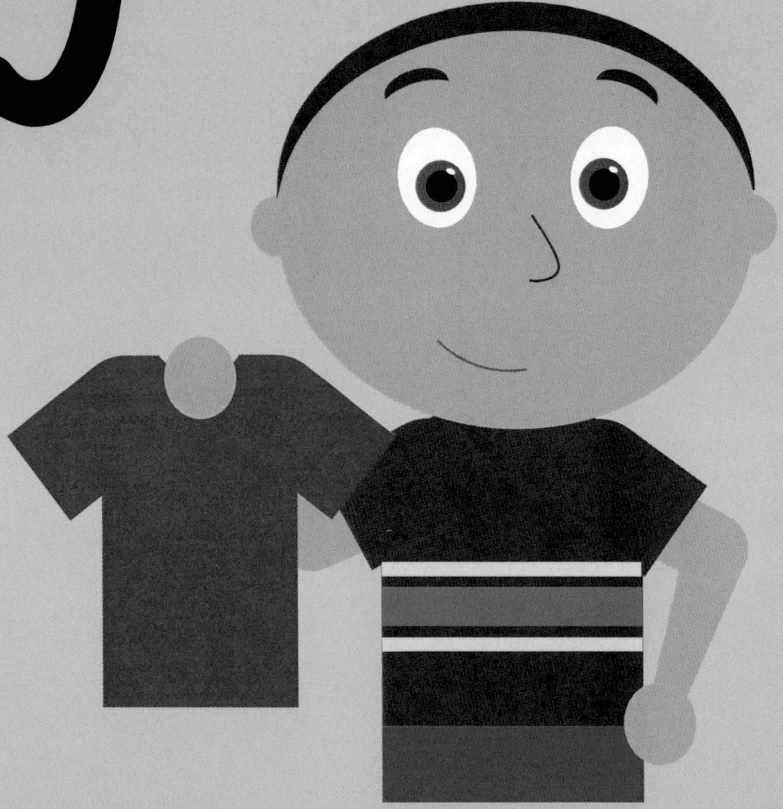

Give a shirt

H h

Horse shirt

Ii

I shirt myself

Jj

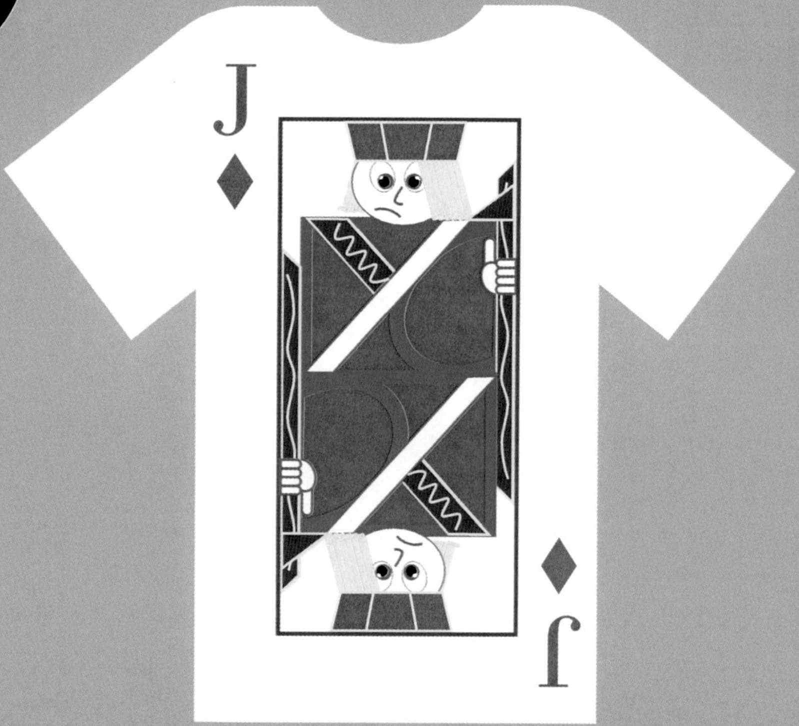
J
J

Jack shirt

Kk

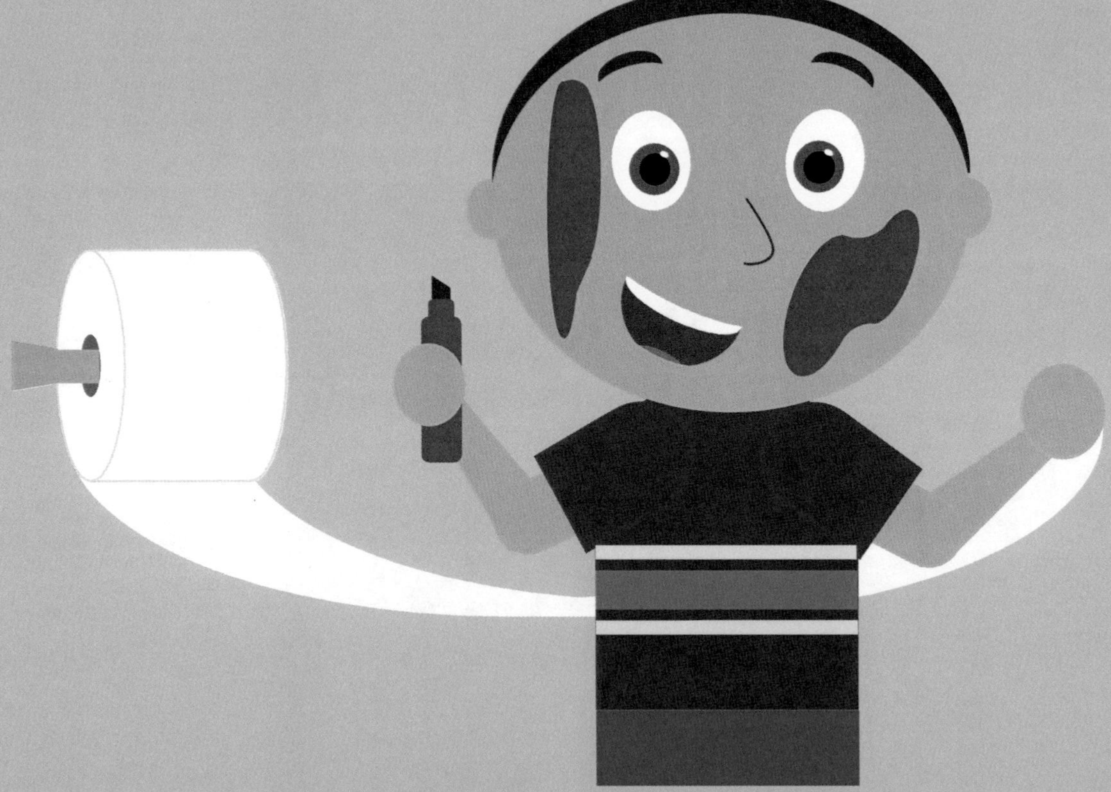

Shirt-y **K**ids

Ll

Shirt **L**oad of **L**aundry

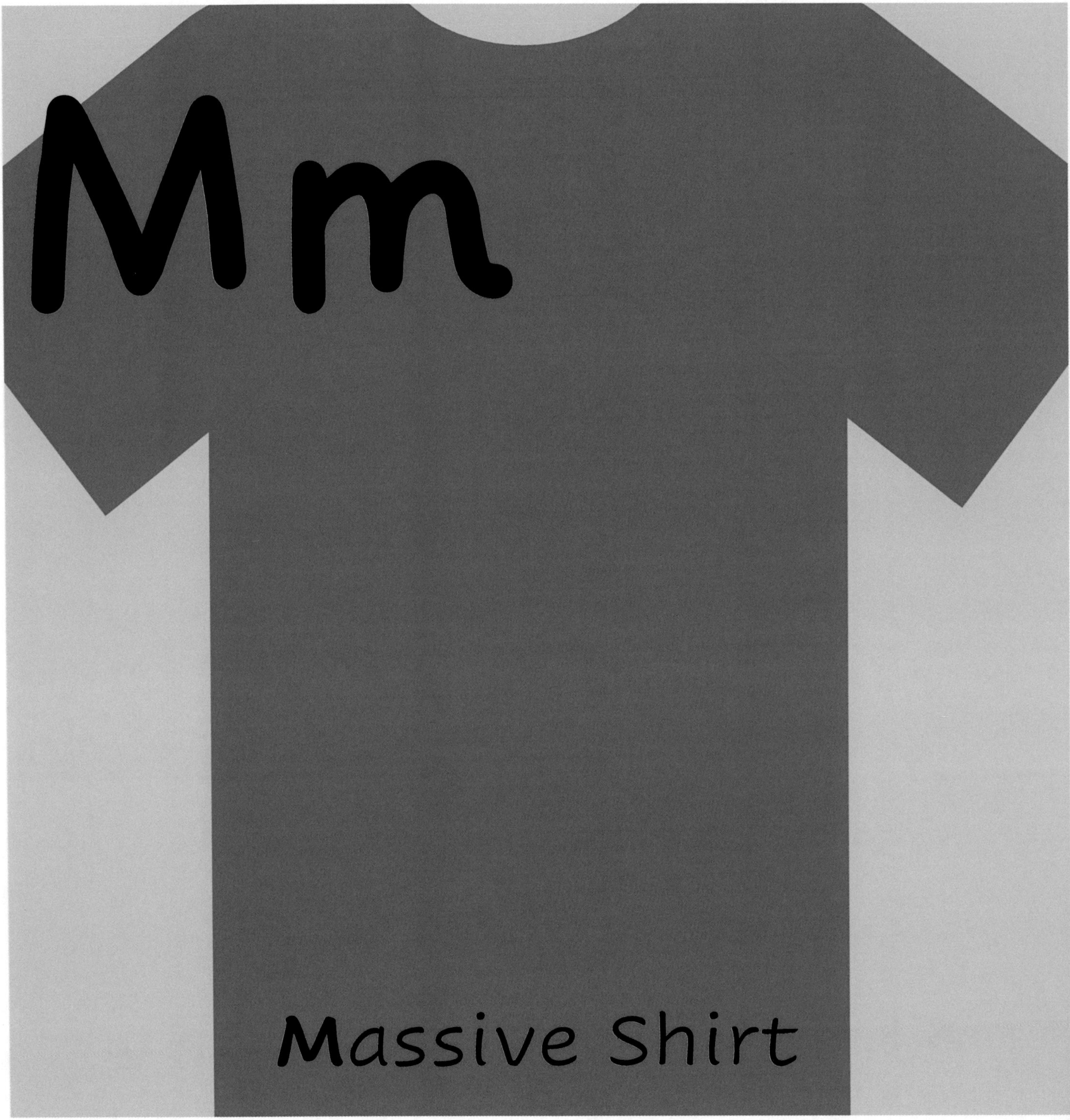
Mm
Massive Shirt

Nn

Nice Shirt

Oo

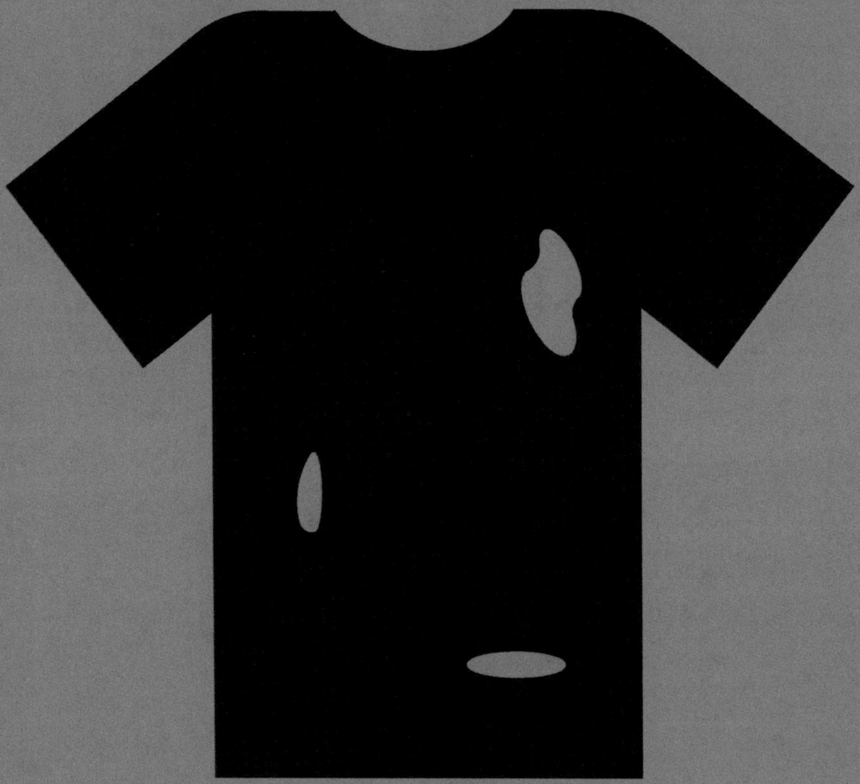

Old Shirt

Pp

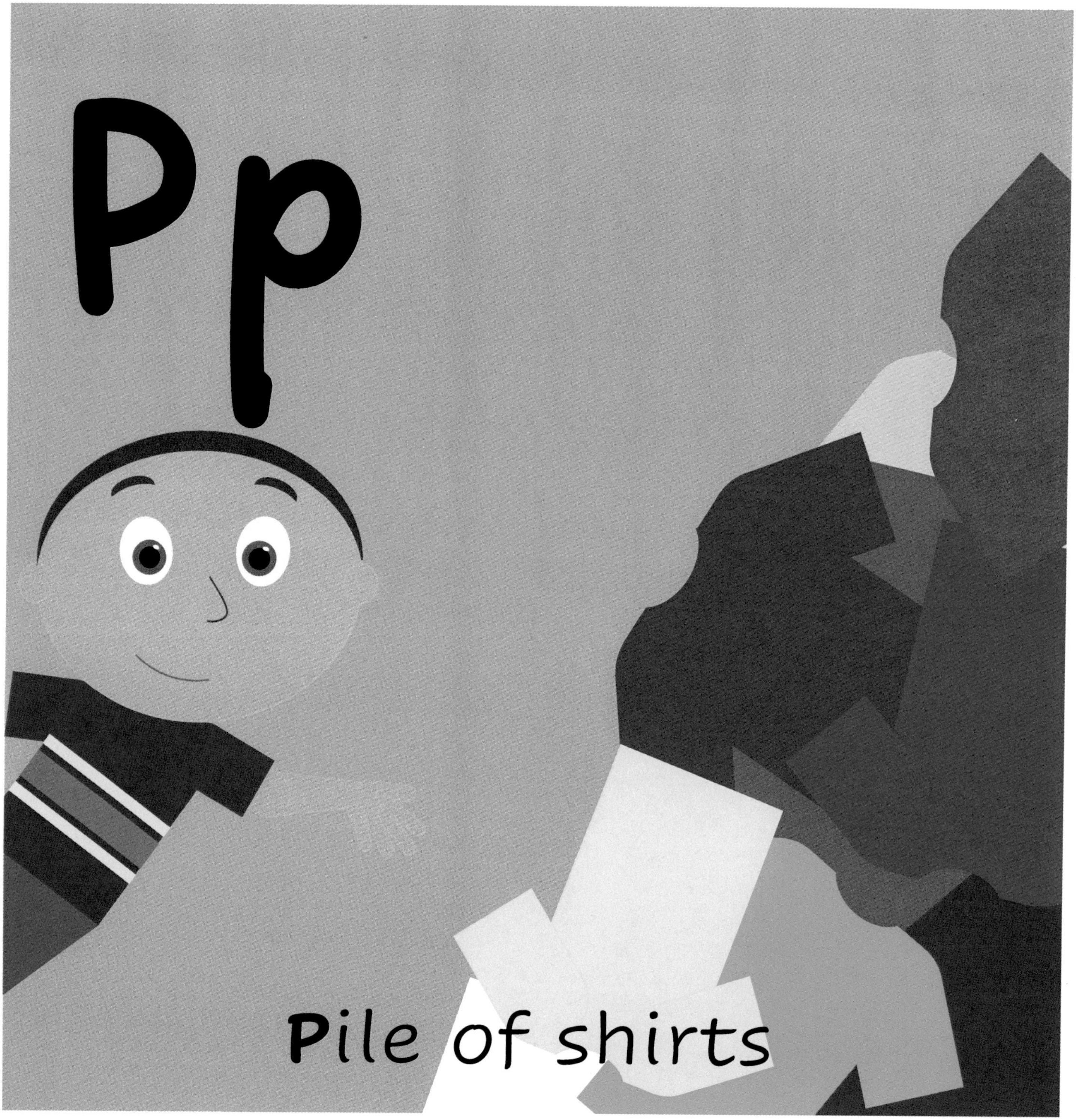

Pile of shirts

Qq

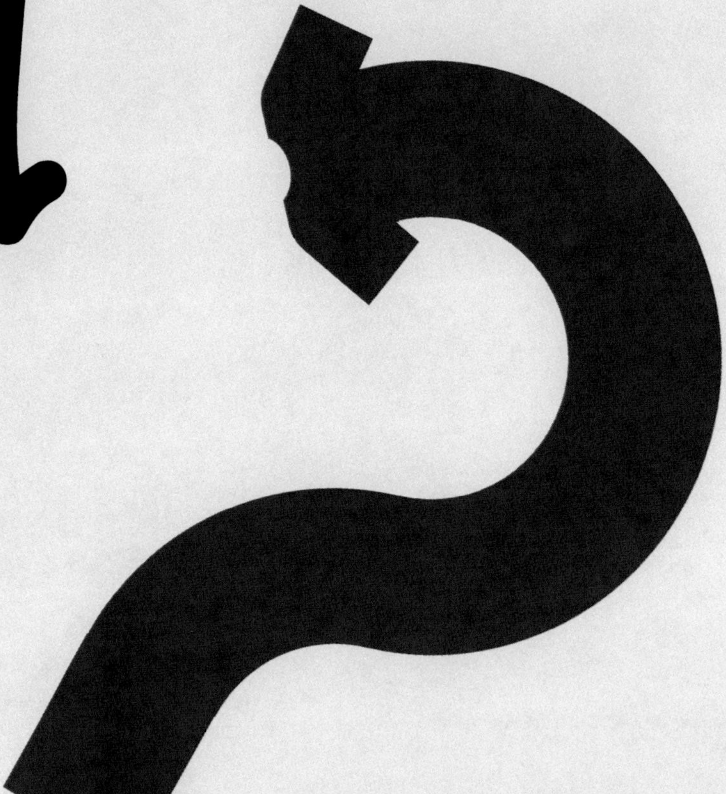

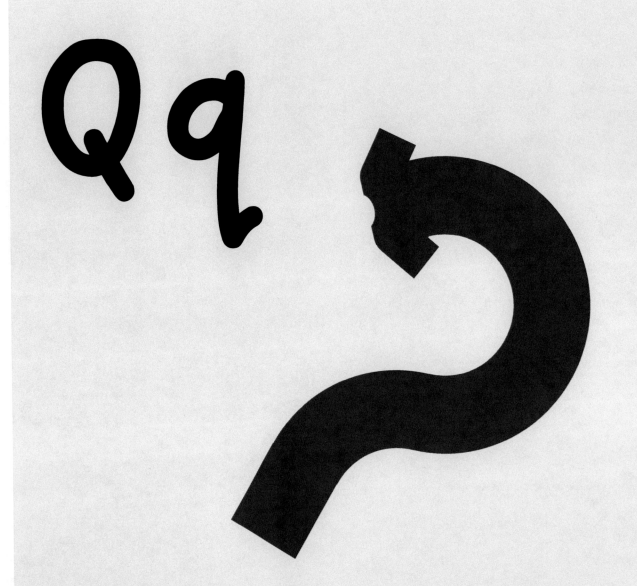

Question mark shirt

Rr

_____
_____
_____

Runny shirt

Ss

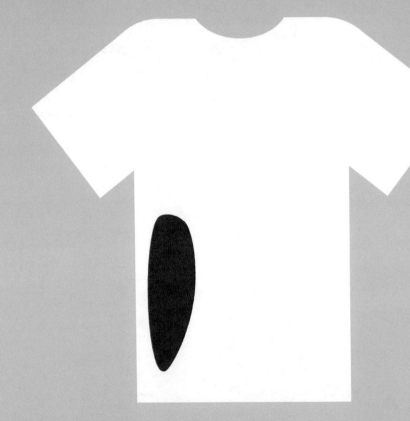

Shirt Stain

Tt

Take a shirt

Uu

Shirt Creek

Up Shirt Creek

Vv

very long shirt

Ww

Bear shirt in the **W**oods

Xx

Xerus shirt

Yy

Shirt **Y**ourself

Zz

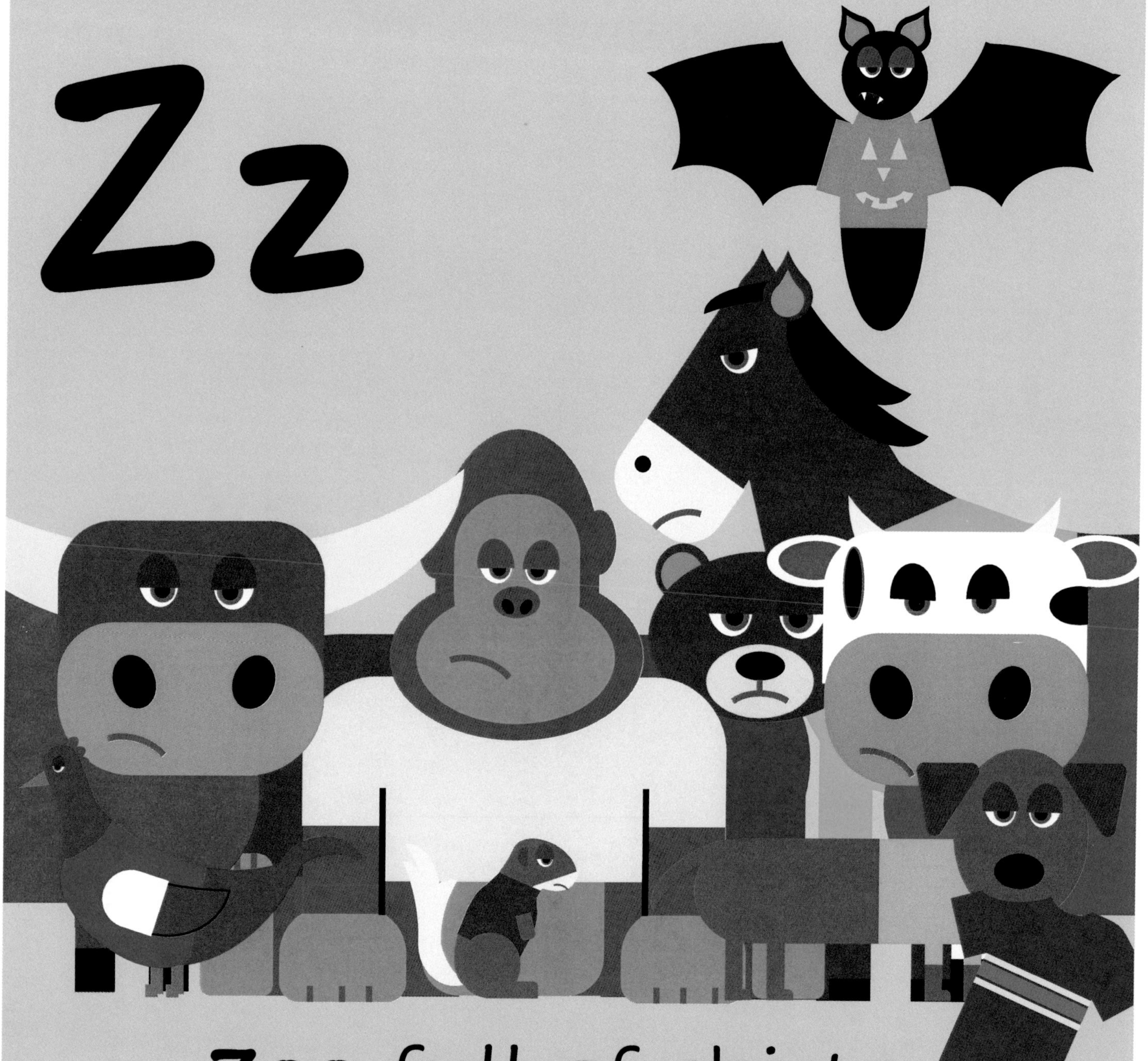

Zoo full of shirts.

Made in the USA
Coppell, TX
31 May 2023

17517825R00019